To Phil.

Hidden Depths:
Payback Time

Simon Williams

by Simon Williams

**Hidden Depths:
Payback Time**

ISBN: 978-1-907540-94-3

Published October 2013

Printed and Published by Anchorprint Group Limited
www.anchorprint.co.uk

Acknowledgements

I would like to dedicate this book to all my children: Amanda, Will, Nicole and Sam and to Dominic and David who sadly never had the chance to grow up but are always in my heart. Also, to my grandchildren Zack and Ella. My dear Mam, Margaret, and my dad Keith who taught me so much in life. My Aunty Pat and Uncle Martin who trusted me and have a special place in my heart. Also my brothers Mark and David.

I would like to thank my proof reader, Roz Sant Henson for all the hard work you put into this book; I am truly grateful.

To the special person who encouraged me to write this book and gave me the inspiration, you know who you are.x

To my number one fan, Julie Oakley, the braveness and courage you are showing makes me your number one fan.

To all the lads on community payback on a Sunday you know who you are. And finally to the proud people of my home city of Salford this book is dedicated to you.

Chapter 1-Justice

I don't know what you're doing as you settle down to read this. Maybe you are sat on the bus going home after work. Maybe you are in bed, or maybe you're at the launderette and killing time waiting for your smalls to dry! What you're going to read is not an everyday mundane tale. It's about the escapades of a Salford lad. I'll fill you in on the story so far. I'm not going to make it complicated. I'll just give you the basics.

The individual is called Williams and comes from the lovely picturesque city that is known as Sunny Salford. You know, the place the BBC relocated to and all its staff literally ran up the M62 with beaming smiles on their faces. Anyway, Williams is basically a good lad but prone to getting himself into a few scrapes. These scrapes stem from a few hair brained scams that don't always pay off. There's never any harm done to anybody.

We're mates but not the type of mates who meet up for coffee and catch up on what we've been up to. We've made our own paths and have very different lives now but we'll always be mates. Even though I have no faults and am pretty much perfect and he has more faults than a T reg Nissan Micra.

Williams is, I believe, living it up on the proceeds of a recently sold Lowry painting that fortuitously found its way into Williams' mum house. I haven't heard from him for months. To be honest I'm glad about the fact. I've got some much going on in my life at the moment....... So why do I feel there is an empty void?

I own a thriving popular bar in a beautiful part of Spain. My rather handsome fiancé, Jonathan, has his appeal due in a month and the British Consul are saying that Jonathan's chances are looking very good and that they are hopeful of getting his conviction overturned. I hear you ask what his conviction was for. Well, I will tell you. It was for the smuggling of stolen diamonds. The fact that he was an ex member of the Greater Manchester Constabulary made quite a few tabloid headlines, I can tell you. The fact that he had been framed, however, didn't make quite the same amount of coverage.

Hopefully, we will be back together soon in the bar we own jointly and doing what we do best; being the ideal hosts.

The last nine months have been the worst of my life. Not because my fiancé has been away from me and a woman has needs, but because I have realised what I could have had.

Williams hasn't even had the decency to keep in touch. The last I heard was when I received his last letter about the sale of the Lowry and an accompanying package containing his Wonderman comics. I haven't heard a dicky bird about him and for Williams to be out of the limelight something cannot be right. Nobody has seen or heard from him; not even his mates.

I had to concentrate all my thoughts and efforts on getting Jonathan out. As I left the local prison on my last visit I knew in my heart that it wouldn't be long until we were back together.

The weeks seemed to fly past and before I knew it was the day of the retrial. I took my place in the courtroom which was strangely empty compared to the last time. Jonathan kept glancing towards me trying to give me a reassuring look that everything would be okay and it wouldn't be long until I felt his strong arms around me. The attraction was still very much alive and I was tingling at the thought of the first night we would have once Jonathan was free. I was sure he was thinking the same. He was only a man after all. The only other thing he might have been thinking about was getting retribution for his false imprisonment.

The British Consul had sent over the best barrister that GMP could afford. No doubt aided by the sale of all the contraband they sold on a monthly basis.

The barrister representing Jonathan was going over his evidence and as he addressed the court he told them he was 200% convinced that his client had been set up. As I listened I knew he was right but I could not say anything. Williams knew a lot of shady people and a few of them lived on my doorstep. So, for my own safety, I decided to keep my mouth shut.

The barrister was asking had it been possible that the diamonds had been planted. I knew they had been because the old flower seller who sold us the vase containing the diamonds had seen to that.

The judge summed up all the evidence and admitted that he too had fallen for the unwitting sham of a conviction. At the original trial he had believed that Jonathan (my wonderful, honest Jonathan) could be capable of such an immoral action. After hearing all the evidence he ordered for Jonathan to be released immediately and awarded him fifty thousand Euros as compensation for his false imprisonment. I was overwhelmed with joy and let out an almighty cheer. My Jonathan was free and our lives could begin again. For once in my life I was really happy.

We all made our way back to the bar where it was drinks all round for the defence team as they had done a marvellous job. As I looked at Jonathan I began to think of the turmoil he must have gone through knowing he was innocent and locked up in a hell hole. From now on I was going to pander to his every need.
We closed the bar about one o'clock as the defence team made their way to their hotels. Now it was my time.

We got back to the bar and went upstairs and all I'll say is that I didn't get to sleep that night. Neither did Jonathan. We did it everywhere. The bed, the shower, the balcony and even nipped down to a nearby hotel swimming pool in the middle of the night. The full moon reflected on the water and the scent from the nearby orange trees made the setting about as romantic as it could possibly get. Jonathan's skin glistened after I had trickled a handful of pool water on his shoulder blade and I watched it run down onto his taut chest. You're waiting for more details aren't you? Well, you will wait as long as City fans waited for a trophy. You don't need to know the details but I will tell you that several hours later we were spent like a used box of Vesta matches after gentle but energetic lovemaking. We made 9 and 1/2 weeks look like an episode of a Ready, Steady, Cook.

I awoke late the next morning and made Jonathan a full English breakfast as he need to regain his strength. I had decided to let him tell me about his experience behind bars in his own time. It felt as if we were as one with each other. Physically we fitted together like a jigsaw piece; perfectly slotting in side by side. We had nine months to catch up on and Williams was the last thing on my mind.

Chapter 2-International Playboy

Williams meanwhile was living the life of a Champagne Charlie and thought he was Salford's international playboy. Clubbing it all night and bed all day. A different girl every night and he had no shame about it. He even told them to get themselves a taxi home as he couldn't be bothered getting out of bed.

Williams was wrapped up in his own little world. The planet could have been hit by an asteroid wiping out half the world's population and he wouldn't have even known or more to the point have even cared. He had, as we say in Salford, been on a 'mad 'un'. This comprised of drinking, spending obscene amounts of money on clothes and fast living and frequenting the sort of clubs that require a password on entry and a very full wallet.

This had gone on for months but suddenly Williams' life was going to change in a way that nobody would have expected. Not even him.

His son asked him to go to his parent's evening and to drive him there in his 13 plate Merc so the other kids could see how much cash he had. Due to his windfall, Williams had suddenly acquired a whole new wardrobe including the brand new impeccably cut Armani suit he was wearing and the Italian shoes that had cost him more than all the shoes he had bought in his life, put together.

When he walked into the school hall you could see he was getting several admiring glances from the female teaching staff and a few from the male ones as well. He and his son were going round seeing all the teachers that taught his son. But the only thing that was on Williams' mind was which bird would be lucky tonight. It was then he noticed Diane Dawson whose blonde hair and sultry looks caught his attention. He was more interested in her than what she was saying. He was staring like a gob-smacked teenager on his first date. As she walked away he could not help but notice her stunning curves and the way her bottom moved up and down in unison. She turned round and smiled and the smile said it all. He said to his son: " They weren't like that when I was in school mate!".

His son looked at his dad in disgust. Williams fancied her and was prepared to pull out all the stops to get her. It was then that he noticed one of the school governors and local MP Hazel Mears. His first thought was

" I'd have her doing my expenses and tax returns but maybe she wouldn't be very good at it".

His second thought was:

"I'm sure she wants more than my vote".

She asked how he was doing (as Williams had met her the year before). It was at that point that she mentioned the museum.

" Look Simon", she said, "I've been in a council meeting all day and the museum was the topic of conversation. I know there are a few grants available if you're interested? Phone me tomorrow", she said, passing Williams her number on a piece of paper.

Williams turned to his son and said:

" I told you the ginger ninja fancied me!"

His son just shook his head in disbelief again. Williams thought about what she had said and thought "Yes, that could be a way out" . He thought he could buy the museum, restore it and then give it back to who it really belonged to; the people of Salford. For the first time in months the guilty thoughts he had been having had gone. In his mind he thought "Yes, Will's teacher will be impressed with that!"

The next morning he woke up early and phoned the local MP.

"Listen, I've decided I will meet the council officials for a preliminary meeting with a view to buying it if the price is right", he said. He continued: "So if you can sort out a meeting see if you can sort out some sort of an agreement", to which she replied:

"OK, I will be in touch as soon as possible".

Williams then drove to the park. His mind was racing. At last he had a challenge and he had a way of getting rid of his ill gotten gains, the money that had been tearing him in half with guilt. The meeting had been arranged for the following day. The following day he arrived at the Town Hall ready and eager to hear what they had to say about proposals for the building that had been neglected for so long. When he heard what they said, he could not believe his luck. They were only asking for seventy grand and there were grants available for two hundred and fifty thousand. He worked out it would cost him, at the most, two hundred and fifty thousand to get it back to its former glory as the jewel in Salford's crown. He could see it, the vision of what the building could become.. He was just amazed that the men in suits couldn't. He was wondering what he paid his council tax for. A bunch of pillocks that don't know what they're doing.

He agreed to the purchase and after two weeks and thousands of phone calls to his solicitors, he was the new owner of the museum even though the money had come from the sale of the recently discovered Lowry. The Lowry that Williams had sold at auction. The Lowry that had changed his life.

Chapter 3-Love at first sight

Williams was now thinking straight for the first time since the visit to Sotheby's that had resulted in the sale of the Lowry painting. He was now the proud new owner of the museum and the only choice he had to make now was to decide who was going to carry out the renovation work on the fine old building. He finally decided that it had to be his old employers PLD based on the fact the he knew they did a reasonable (emphasis on the reasonable) job at a decent price.

A meeting was arranged with the directors, the contracts manager (Nick, his cousin) and the works secretary, Sarah Lane. He told them what he wanted doing and how he would pay in three stages. He even put a retention clause in the contract saying that if they overran on the works by one day then they would have to start paying him. How far had he come since the days in the slate shed? The first words out of William's mouth were " Anything that is found is mine and I will look over everything before it goes in the skip" The only thing they found was an old coal carving which Williams gave to his daughter , as she collected things like that.

Williams even took to overseeing the job as he wanted it to be perfect. Work started the following Monday and the workers arrived on site at 7.45am unlike Williams, who strangely enough had taken it upon himself to take his son Will and his daughter Nicole to school (even though they only lived a two minute walk away from the school). He was hoping to catch a glimpse of Will's teacher Diane Dawson. Much to the annoyance of his son as his son didn't want to get teased by his mates. Williams then went home and changed into his work gear.

"God, I heard you got a right result with that picture didn't you?", asked Binnsy.

"Yea", said Williams.

"Heard you've been on a bender for a few months", said young Azza.

"I suppose I have. But I've sorted my head out now", replied Williams.

"What are you up to at weekend?" asked Williams.

"Nothing, why?" , they replied in unison.

"Well, I don't know if you fancy it but I've got a box at Old Trafford now. So, I don't know if you doing anything but we could all go to the game on

Saturday if you want. We could all meet in Eccles at the Town Hall",
Williams informed them.
Trotty then chipped in
"Does that include me? And does that include free beer?"
" Hasn't it always, mate?" , Williams answered him.

The lads started work on Williams' project and Williams was walking
around the site feeling very proud of himself. "Right lads any treasure we
find is mine. Have a good look any anything that looks like shit put to one
side so I can have a good root. You never know what you might find in a
place like this. After looking all day all they found was an old horse carved
out of coal pulling an old cart , Williams thought he would clean it up and
give it to his eldest Amanda as she liked stuff like that , Suddenly, at three
o'clock brew time arrived and Williams rushed home to get changed and
put his Armani suit on and went to pick his children up. His son approached
him in the school yard and it was then that Will said the magic words:
" Dad, I've lost my planner".
"Right, I'd better go and see your teacher then", said Williams smirking.
This was a good excuse to go and see Diane he thought. Williams then
approached his teacher and said:
"Hi, Miss Dawson. I believe my son has lost his planner".
"Yes", she replied in a sexy voice, "but he can get a new one from the
library".
"That's very good of you, Miss Dawson. It is Miss isn't it?", he asked.
"Oh, yes. Very much so. I've been on my own for years", she replied.
"Well, I know this might sound a little forward but I've got tickets for Much
Ado about Nothing at a theatre in Liverpool if you fancy coming", he said to
Diane.
" Oh, Simon. The pleasure would be all mine", she replied.
" Well, that's great. If you fancy it I've got tickets for the United and
Liverpool game the day after if you'd like to go to that", he added.
"Well, I don't know about staying over but I'd love to go to the game but let
me think about it", she said excitedly.

Chapter 4-The Date

Williams was now excited as he waited for his date to arrive and when he saw her approaching, he was not disappointed. Diane looked stunning. She wore a dress that showed off her curves to their maximum potential. The drive to Liverpool was full of non stop chat as they both seemed to have so much in common. They both shared a love of football and it seemed to Williams that his luck might be in as she decided to bring her overnight bag .

They walked into the hotel where she was impressed by the old building's interior and it was then after Williams had signed in and they reached their room that she was amazed by the bouquet of flowers that were waiting for her. She picked up the card attached to the flowers that said:
Thank you so much for being my date. Let's hope we have a great weekend. She was impressed, as any woman would be.
As time was pushing on they had to leave the hotel room no sooner than they arrived as the play was about to start at The Empire. Williams and Diane went into the theatre where they were greeted by the usher who showed them to their seats. Diane wasn't disappointed as Williams had spared no expense with the tickets. The only problem for Williams was the twenty two stone woman who was sat right in front of him who was leaning back on her seat which was pushing against Williams' knees and making him feel annoyed and uncomfortable, which he did not want to say as he was trying desperately to impress Diane. Williams was puzzled as to how she got in that seat in the first place as she resembled a sumo wrestler. They only thing that was stopping him from saying anything was the thought that if she punched him she would probably knock him into next week.
At the interval, the drinks were waiting for them and Williams' thoughts were that he would have to change seats with Diane without her noticing. After their drinks , they returned to their seats, Williams made the fatal mistake of opening the door for Diane. He knew then that Diane would head back to her original seat and Williams would find himself squashed up being the sumo woman again. Being a gentleman, for once, had not paid off. He was going to be sat behind Tubby for the rest of the show. Mind

you, it's not as though he had a clue what the play was about anyway. He was just going to impress his new date.

The play ended with Diane thoroughly enjoying her evening and Williams made out that he had too. They then went back to the Adelphi where Williams had booked the VIP cocktail lounge for them both. After trying every cocktail on the card and talking about how enjoyable the evening had been they decided to retire to their palatial suite.

Williams was quickly under the sheets as soon as Diane said she was going to go to the bathroom and get more comfortable. Within minutes Williams was amazed at the sight that greeted him when the bathroom door opened. The bed sheet that Williams was lying under suddenly raised so it resembled a wigwam. Tender kisses turned into passionate embraces. It was then that Diane turned to Williams and said:

" Have you got any protection?"

" I've never paid for protection in my life. I'm from Salford, love. Have some respect!", Williams replied.

"No, You know what I mean. Stop being silly", she said.

"Yes, I know what you mean. No, I haven't" , he answered her.

"Well, you better get something then or you're not coming near me", she told him.

Williams then quickly got dressed back into his suit and raced out of the hotel as fast as his legs would carry him. He has seen an all night chemist on their way back from the theatre and thought he would try there first. On finding the chemist he went up to the man behind the counter and said in the thickest of Salford accents:

" Have you got any Johnnies mate?"

The man behind the counter replied:

" Been in court pal and missed your train?"

"No, mate. What makes you think that?", Williams asked.

"You're a Manc with a suit on!!", the man said.

"No, mate, I'm from Salford. And anyway less of the humour, Tarbuck!" Williams said taunting him before adding:

" And give me a packet of 12", he said (Truthfully,he thought he would be lucky if he actually got round to using one).

" £12.60 please, mate" , the man said.

"£12.60! You must have seen me coming", shouted Williams. Unlike Diane who was now snoring away under the crisp white sheets back at the hotel.

Williams, at this point, was walking as fast as he could back to the Adelphi hotel. He walked into the room where Williams saw Diane sleeping soundly, and oblivious to everything in the luxurious bed. This wasn't exactly going to plan he thought to himself. Williams sat down in the chair thinking it could only happen to him.

Williams then raided the mini-bar and shoved a few extra bottles into his case without realising he would be charged when he checked out of his room.

The following morning Williams was awoken by the sound the shower as he slept in the chair.

Williams followed suit and went for his shower after Diane had finished in the bathroom. He quickly showered and dressed in the clothes he had chosen to wear for the match which consisted of trainers, Gucci jeans, Stone Island jacket and jumper and although he was the wrong side of 48 he wore a baseball cap. Who on earth did he think he was?

They left the hotel and took the five minute walk to the ground walking hand in hand laughing about the evening before. They soon arrived at Anfield and made their way through the turnstiles. Once inside they found their seats in the area allocated for the United fans. However, Williams, somehow, became a changed person once he started to soak up the atmosphere of the stadium . This metamorphosis seemed to come about when, purely by chance, he bumped into four of his mates; Les Batty, Mitch and the Hart brothers, Steve and Alan. Suddenly, the sophisticated man from the night before disappeared before Diane's very eyes. He quickly fell back into his old routine of being the most annoying fan in the stadium (regardless of who you supported) and singing every single word from every single chant that the crowd shouted. Swear words included. Williams didn't care who was sitting next to him, not even his date . The same date that last night he had tried so much to impress. Williams was now in his glee.

The final minutes of the game were now drawing in and the game was still stalemate at 0-0. Williams was screaming like a banshee at the United team trying to spur them on to victory. At the United end, things were looking good. Rooney, complete with his latest weave, was in the box and flicked the ball to Van Persie who rounded the Liverpool defender and blasted the ball into the top right hand corner of the net. The jubilant Van Persie ran over to the away fans and celebrated directly in front of them. Williams looked at his date and then glanced at Van Persie. There was only going to be one winner. Before Diane even had chance to ask what he was doing, Williams was on the pitch celebrating with Van Persie and the rest of the United players. That was however, until the match stewards ran on the pitch and dragged Williams kicking and screaming to the ground's holding cells. Williams would be having another day in court the following day.

Diane meanwhile was left to make the five minute walk back to the hotel on her own. She was not a happy bunny. Williams was probably safer locked up in a cell in Liverpool than he would be in Diane's company. She was raging and her strides became faster and more urgent as she walked back.

On arriving back at the hotel and reaching the room she had shared with Williams, she immediately pulled every single head off the bunch of flowers and threw them in the bin. All this time she muttered something about Williams being fatherless.

She then packed her overnight bag, jumped into a taxi to Lime Street Station and booked a one way ticket to Manchester. She was fuming. She was going to make him pay for the humiliation.

She was still no happier the following day when she was calling out the register in school when she came to Will Williams' name.

"Yes, miss", answered Will, to which Diane replied:

"Detention. One hour!"

Why, miss?", asked Will.

"Don't argue. Or else it will be two!", Diane told him. Will was totally bewildered as he didn't know why he had to attend a detention. He had never even been to detention before. But Diane knew. And so would Williams when he next picked his son up.

Meanwhile, back in Liverpool, at the city's magistrates' court, Williams was up before the judge where he was given a 3 year banning order for pitch encroachment. This meant he couldn't attend any matches home or away. He was also given a £400 fine and sixty hours community payback.

He was not a happy man, especially when he eventually got back to The Adelphi and he was informed that he was being charged another day's charge for storing his clothes in the room he had booked for himself and Diane.

He realised that the days of taking his two children on the two minute drive to school were probably over as Diane would never want to see him again. However, what he did learn from the whole weekend was that he needed to get a vasectomy.

Chapter 5-The Clinic

Williams arrived at the museum the following day at seven thirty in the morning. He was greeted by a cheerful looking Trotty who said to him:
" I saw you with Van Persie, mate. How much did the pleasure cost you?"
"Four hundred quid fine , three year banning order and sixty hours walking round with one of them jackets Tevez had to wear, mate", Williams replied before adding, " Only I'll have to pay all my hours back!".
"So, what does that involve then?", asked Trotty.
"I don't know, mate. I've got to go and see the probation officer next Sunday", Williams informed him before adding:
" By the way, I've got some good news for you Trotty".
"Oh yea. What's that then? Am I getting a pay rise?"
" No mate, You know that box I got at Old Trafford? You can have it now for you and three others because I can't go can I? Just make sure you share it out equally between all the lads now and again", said Williams.
"Oh, thanks a lot, mate. Your loss is my gain! Oh, I forgot to ask you. How did the date go?" asked Trotty.
"Well. It was much ado about nothing really, mate!", he replied. " I don't think she was too keen when I was cuddling Van Persie instead of her. But I tell you what I have decided over the weekend, mate", said Williams.
"What? " asked Trotty.
"I'm going to get the snip! I spent all bloody night trying to buy condoms. At my age! By the time I got back she was asleep", Williams replied. For once Trotty didn't quite know what to say.
" Bit drastic isn't it, mate?", he asked.
"No, it isn't. I'm not going to get caught out like that again! I consider it an investment, mate", Williams explained. He then walked away asking Trotty if he ever going to do any work. How the tables had turned.
He then phoned the clinic in the nearby leafy suburb of Worsley and booked his appointment for 10 .0'clock the following morning having never been so sure about anything before.
For the remainder of the day, Williams talked about how he had got to celebrate with Van Persie and how he had been taken off the pitch by the rather irate stewards.. His mate Binnsy turned round and said:
" I saw you on Sky! Bet your date wasn't best pleased! How did it go? You said she was a right stunner".

" No woman on Sky!", replied Williams doing his best to imitate Bob Marley but failing dismally. "Van Persie, mate! I don't think it gets much better than that!" said Williams. Binnsy walked away shaking his head not quite believing that Williams was capable of causing a commotion wherever he went.

The following morning, Williams walked into the private health clinic. He had parked up in the beautifully landscaped car park and made his way through the automatic doors which led to the main reception. He was amazed at was he seeing. Everything was brand new and spotless. There were potted palms everywhere (and not those plastic ones you see in offices covered in dust where the cleaners just couldn't be bothered cleaning them) with fresh flowers on the counter top. It was like the entrance to a five star hotel.

After telling the receptionist his name and a quick phone call, a nurse appeared and led him to a nearby room where she asked him to get changed into a gown and lie on the bed. She left the room and he quickly did as he was told wondering if he was doing the right thing. He lay there for a couple of minutes wondering just how sure he was going to be when, to his horror, in walked a familiar face. It was Nurse Hookway who Williams knew from his many previous visits to Salford Royal Hospital. She was destined to follow Williams wherever his medical needs took him. She smiled and said:

" Hi, Simon. Still single? I heard about the painting. Sold it for a right few quid didn't you?"

"Yes, I did", Williams replied. "And I heard you were in Walton, nursing scousers".

" No. Changed my mind and went private instead. Anyway, lift your gown up", she said to Williams.

"What?", shrieked Williams.

"Come on. Be a brave boy! I won't be seeing anything I haven't seen before", said Nurse Hookway.

"Oh, don't be so sure about that, love!", Williams informed her.

" Oh, believe me, Mr Williams. I have seen it before. If I remember rightly I gave you a bed bath at least four times when you were in your coma on my ward. And honestly Mr Williams, I wouldn't advise you to leave your cruet set to medical science!", said Nurse Hookway in a tone that was as dry as an unbuttered cream cracker.

Williams had never felt so embarrassed in all his life. Well, he had . Maybe once or twice. He remained silent and decided to get it all over with as quickly as possible.

Within minutes, his undercarriage resembled a bald turkey's neck with two dangling cannon balls. He was then led to a crisp, freshly made bed and asked to lie down. In agony, he lay down and remained motionless while the Nurse Hookway and a young student nurse called Amena pulled up his gown and smiled. Nurse Hookway was finding it hard to hide the fact that this was one of the most satisfying days in her nursing career. For once, Williams was speechless and not asking for anything.

He knew that the part of his anatomy that he referred to as "THE GOVERNOR" would never be the same again.

Nurse Amena was talking to Williams in an attempt to make him relax while Nurse Hookway was saying things like:

" I suppose I'd better sell my shares in the pram shop on the precinct".

After a few minutes Williams was relaxed. His mind began to wander. Two women checking him over while he was rooted to the spot. " I bet this would cost a few quid in Amsterdam!", he thought to himself.

After an hour and a half of having his balls played with, they then told him that they were finished. He was told he could return to his room, have a cup of tea and when he felt okay to go home he was free to go. Finally Nurse Hookway added:

"We'll get in touch by post with details of your check up appointment. You will have to return in six weeks. Take this sample pot so you can fill it up and it can be tested during the appointment".

Williams asked for a bigger pot.

Nurse Hookway ignored him and tutted before leaving the room.

Chapter 6-Chaos

Here in Malaga,Williams could not have been further from my mind. The museum, although part of my childhood, meant very little to me now. I had, like many other people, grown up spending many days (and evenings for that matter) in Buile Hill Park. Playing on the pitch and putt, spending hours just messing around in the greenhouse listening to the mynah birds getting them to say rude words. The trouble was they already knew every swear word in the English language. If the kids in Salford has spent as much time learning as they did teaching those birds to swear, then I'm sure much more graffiti would be spelt correctly. But those halcyon days of playing in the park were in the past and I had a new life in a new country.
Jonathan and I had been back behind the bar together for 2 months and we were happier than ever. The summer season was in full swing and the theme nights and happy hours we had introduced had started to attract tourists in their droves. A little bit of me thinks it may have been to do with Jonathan's notoriety and people just wanted to be nosey but to be honest I didn't care. If it helped bring in the punters it was a bonus.
The weather was perfect. The days were hot and the skies were a brilliant blue and the nights were balmy with a soft breeze which always seemed to encourage lovemaking. Well, I think it was a mixture of that and the local plonk which the tourists seemed to drink like it was council pop.
Life couldn't get any better. Jonathan had his compensation from his wrongful imprisonment and we had invested it in the bar. We had a new boiler fitted as the old one was very temperamental and we had a new larger, kidney shaped bath fitted because ...well, I prefer to keep the reasons to myself thank you. I'll just say that bath times lasted longer than they did before. I had started to feel that Jonathan no longer associated me with Williams and he had started to love me for who I was. I was now his Sharon.
So, you can imagine that life was good. It was a bit like Shirley Valentine only I hadn't left anyone behind and it wasn't Tom Conti that I was making love to every night. It was Jonathan and I wouldn't have changed him for anything.
I hadn't thought about life in Salford once in those past few months until one day a group of tourists came in and I instantly recognised one of the

women from my school days. I didn't know any of them particularly well but we always feel an affiliation with people from our home town don't we? Wherever we are in the world if we meet a group of people and they're from the North, we feel we should talk to them rather than the Southerners don't we? Even if the group of Northerners are the biggest load of knobheads you have ever met in your life. We tend to give fellow Northerners the benefit of the doubt.

Well, intuition said this crowd were salt of the earth and what's more they would put money in the till. These looked like 20 pints and a dozen triple Malibu and coke sort of girls (and that was each, not between them).

They came into the bar on what was a busy evening. The bar was full but the atmosphere was relaxed. Customers were mixing with people they didn't know. Chatting about life and what made them happy and it made me feel lucky to be alive. This is why I loved the place.

I went over to say hello to the woman I had recognised when the group had entered the bar. I smiled and asked:

"Don't I know you from school?"

"I thought I knew your face!", shouted the woman I had remembered.

"Is it Sharon ?", the woman asked.

"Yes, although I answer to Shazza when I'm in Salford!", I answered her laughing. "I'm so sorry I just can't remember your name", I added.

"My name's Jackie Froggat. But everyone called me Froggy at school!",the woman answered.

"Oh, yes. I think I remember you. Anyway I'd like to get you all a drink on the house. And it will only be the one mind. I remember saying the same to Williams' mum when he came to visit but she had said "Oh, that's very nice of you! I'll have a triple brandy chaser please". Jackie, however just asked for San Miguel all round and said thanks. We reminisced about school days and how life had changed. It was after Jackie had made a comment about having to have 4 different bins outside your house and it being a logistical nightmare putting the right bin out on the right day that she made a passing comment about Buile Hill museum being bought.

"Oh, who's bought it?", I asked.

"Do you remember Simon Williams from school ? He's bought it. I heard, between you, me and the gate post, that it's some sort of gesture to the people of Salford. He's quite some playboy now I hear. Flash suits, fancy car and all that", Jackie said, unaware that I knew him like the back of my hand.

"Oh, really!", I replied. " I think I do remember him. Well, I hope he knows what's he's doing", I said, trying to appear to be totally disinterested while all the time being totally shocked at his grand gesture.

As the night got busier I had to leave their company to serve behind the bar but as 10 0 clock approached the group of women made their way over and said they were leaving to go to a nearby nightclub. I said goodbye and waved them off.

Over the course of the week, the girls came in every night and I can say without a doubt the bar's takings went up steadily night by night. Diane, Kathy and Moe drank like fish but gradually they became part of the fixtures and fittings. So much so, that as they said goodbye on the last day I said to Jackie:

"Look, Jackie. I'm getting married in two months. It'd be great if you could come back over for it. Drinks will all be on the house".

"Oh, don't worry about that love. We'll go anywhere for a free piss up! Count us in!", she replied.

And with that they made their way down the street into the glorious sunshine to make the most of the last day in Spain and I got back to serving drinks and making plans for what was going to be the happiest day of my life.

Chapter 7-Litter picking

The day arrived that Williams had to attend Salford probation office to do his payback, which to Williams was going to be an eye-opener ,they asked him what skills he had. He didn't want to mention about previous attempts to grow plants ,as he thought they would have him digging and working hard . Thinking on his feet,Williams told them he was a chef. Winter was drawing in and he didn't want to be cold when he could be in a kitchen , warm and healthy. The supervisor gave Williams an orange jacket and said "We are litter picking on duchy fields". Williams was in shock. He lived not five minutes from there. It didn't take long until word got out where he was . A taxi driver, Peter Kay, pulled up alongside him and shouted "Williams you knob head". Williams just put his head down . Then the supervisor was confronted by a man who Williams knew (for legal reasons can't say his name) "Knock his hours mate,and you pick that litter up not them". Williams wanted to die. Within the space of ten minutes he had seen three people he knew and they were all taking the mickey out of him . Williams turned to his mate George Earnshaw and said "It doesn't get much lower than this does it mate? We got to get in them kitchens with Wes Mcgill. Don't worry mate, I got a plan that will get us in there next week .Just watch and learn mate". Williams then went to the supervisor and said "Look mate, I am from round here and its not on. I don't mind litter picking but I don't think its fair when everyone seems to know me or George".The supervisor agreed as he was getting sick of being beeped at and being shouted abuse at by William's mates ,who thought it was funny to follow him round and drop their crisp packets .The following week they had been moved to the kitchens .His plan had worked. George was buzzin as he liked nothing better than talking and Wes was made up as he had two helpers who knew what they were doing .... well George did Williams just went round with a teaspoon tasting everything thing like he was Gordon Ramsay. "More salt Wes" or "More sugar", when tasting the custard .In charge of the kitchens was the supervisor, Little Lil. She was well liked by all the lads as she was firm but fair. Williams and George would say daft things to her all day long , but she just ignored them. Tragedy was about to strike for Williams. His mate, Wes the chef, was due to finish his hours and Willliams was now to take his place as the head chef. Little Lil thought Williams was a top chef and so did he in his own little world. Well, one day he was put in charge he thought this is easy. We will make a 'lobby' If you don't know what that is, it's a stew with a crust on and they have it in Wigan. Williams was throwing all the ingredients in the pan and the stew was tasting lovely ,when Little Lil said "Where has the swede gone?" To which Williams replied "In the stew, why? " " You don't have lobby with swede in! " , said Little Lil . "You do today! " said Williams. " No you don't and get it out !!" snapped Lil. Two of the lads in the kitchen, Rob and Dan Hindle proceeded to sieve all the swede out as that was for the normal veg. Gordon Ramsey wasn't having a good day , but the stew tasted great and Williams knew it. He had used a secret recipe that he had found in an old cook book . He had made so much that the whole kitchen was eating it bowl after bowl. Much to the annoyance of Little Lil. She told Williams to "Stop telling them to taste it or there would be none left!! " . "No problem, Lil. There is there loads left I've made sure of that ".Williams was now getting the jist of the kitchens and knew his and George s payback would fly by ……………….

Chapter 8-Blue rinse Mafia

Williams arrived at the museum early the next morning to be greeted by Trotty who said:

" Had a great time at the match on Saturday. how was your payback mate?". "Sound" said Williams, not wanting to tell him about the swede. Besides, he wouldn't have a clue what lobby was ,as it was a Wigan dish and Williams didn't have the energy to tell him. "So we can't follow you around Dawny's Hills while you're picking litter up then?" . "No mate, I'm in the kitchens now and it's a good laugh I can tell you , there are a few PLD there as well but I can't say who. So don't ask mate! What was old Trafford like?Them meals are bang on aren't they?" . "Yeah really enjoyed it thanks" said Trotty. Williams grinned. " Don't thank me, thank Van Persie. He's the reason you got the box. Oh and Liverpool magistrates court. Tell you what mate I'm really impressed with the way this jobs going and on time isn't it ?"

"Yeah mate, Higgins has seen to that .He said you put a retention clause on the job. Is that right? Asked Trotty. "Yeah mate. I want to make sure its done on time". It was then that Binnsy and Azza arrived on the job , Binnsy said "You seen all the plod out there?". " No. Wonder what they want?" said Trotty. Suddenly, like a scene from The Sweeney, the police stormed into the museum, shouting the words that Williams would never forget. " Mr Williams I am arresting you for the theft of the Lowry painting, The Factory Gates. You don't have to say anything but what you do say will be taken down and used in evidence against you " Trotty. Phone my solicitor mate and tell him to meet me there". With this Williams was led into a waiting police van.

 Within minutes of arriving at the local nick, Williams was led into a cell ,where he would have to wait until his solicitor arrived. After an hour of sitting waiting, he was shown to the interview room , where the two policemen sat across the desk from him. "Good morning. I am DS Robert Jones and with me is my colleague, PC Alan Burke ,

It has come to our attention that you have recently sold a Lowry painting, 'The Factory Gates', for half a million pounds. Is that true?".

"No. I got five hundred and twenty thousand pounds mate" , said Williams The two policemen looked at one another.

"So you are admitting it then?" said the detective

"Admitting what? " said Williams

"That you sold it? " confirmed the DS Jones.

"Yes I sold it. Why, What's the problem?" said Williams with an innocent expression.

"Because it was stolen" chipped in PC Burke.

"No it wasn't "said Williams. Sounding almost wounded by their accusation.

"Well tell us where you got it from then?" said the DS Jones growing more impatient by the minute.

" I got it from my Mam. She got it from Mick the pot man. The one with the dangling earring. He has a stall on Salford Flea market on a Thursday. Look, what have I done wrong? and why are you wasting my time?" asked a very indignant Williams.

The two policemen looked at one another and PC Burke replied

"We have evidence to prove that either you, or someone you know, stole that painting".

"Whatever " said Williams casually.

It was with this that Williams s solicitor said "can you tell me what the charge is? My client has been forthcoming. So why is he here?"

With this the two police left the room for ten minutes while Williams and his solicitor talked. "They've got nothing on you here Si. "I know that, Mike. I'll be home in ten. Ha, the muppets ".

No sooner had said this then he was walking out, laughing and on his way back to the museum. However thirty minutes later, Williams would hear news that would leave him fuming.

Williams phone rang exactly half an hour after he had arrived back at the museum. It was Sandra." Look Simon. The police are at your Mam's and they are arresting her for the theft of the Lowry " "OK Sandra, I'll be there as quick as I can" said Williams. Five minutes later he was in the street where a crowd of his Mam's mates had gathered. The Blue Rinse Mafia as Williams called them. He could hear an irate Mrs Williams shouting "Don't forget my dogs!!! " as she was being led into the van. The police had to get a special van for Buster and Murphy as she wouldn't go anywhere without them .Ann Keogh and the rest of the Blue Rinse Mafia where banging on the van stopping the van from going anywhere. The police were on their radio calling for back up as the scenes were getting ugly. Even the Salford Pigeon was in the sky radioing down the manic scenes. Mrs Williams was driven at alarming speed to the precinct police station. Outside the station there was a large mob gathering. Word had spread that an OAP had been arrested for the theft of the Lowry. Even Tony Flynn from Salford on line had turned up to interview the locals. All this commotion was going on outside, unbeknown to Mrs Williams, who was busy inside cleaning the cells. They were filthy! Williams had sent his solicitor in to get his Mam out .He would make sure she would be out as quickly as possible. It was even reported that the Gala Bingo , next door, was shut for the first time ever. Tony Flynn approached Williams and said "Is it true they have arrested your mam over the painting?" Williams replied " yeah mate. A gross miscarriage of justice and I will get to the bottom of this. Trust me." "Well, we are live on line. Is there anything you would like to add? " asked Flynn the reporter. " Yeah, there is. Who In there right mind would arrest a seventy two year old woman for this? "and quickly added " I would like to thank all the people of Salford for coming out to show your support. I don't think it will be long before she is out and back at home. Thank you and no further comment". Meanwhile, inside the station Mike Rainford was working his magic. The interview consisted of Mrs Williams following the age old tactic of "No comment" She knew it had served her sons well in the past , 30 minutes later and the police were still no nearer to finding out who stole the painting. Mrs Williams was released on bail. There were huge cheers from the crowd (some might say mob) outside. It was just then when Williams received a text from the clinic saying his sample was due for testing within the hour. As you blokes would say, he had to knock one out and get to Worsley within the hour. He raced home and got his mags out and read his favourite story. Five minutes later, the large jam jar was filled. I'm sure he didn't need that much but it was a good story! He raced from his house to the clinic and when he got there , he realised he was ten minutes too late. He turned to the lady on reception and said , "Listen love, I live too far away to get here in 10 minutes. Is there any where I can go in here?". To which nurse Amena politely said "Yes sir we do have a room for that". "Oh great" said Williams "You can show me and do it for me, if you like? " . She looked at Williams with disgust and said "No thank you Sir. There are magazines in there and a 70 inch flat screen with a remote and no shortage of DVDs. Williams thought, not for the first time in his life, that he had died and gone to heaven. He sat on the comfy leather settee and looked at the mags . He realised that these were the hardest core mags he had ever seen. He then pressed the remote and even he was shocked at what he was seeing. Williams was in his glee. Just then, he had a thought..." I hope no one is filming this!!" . The film was the hardest of the hard and it didn't take him long. Pot filled to the brim, he walked out bold as brass and said " I'll see you tomorrow. Same time OK girls?" They laughed. Williams then went straight round to his Mam's where she was sat having a cup of tea,as if nothing had happened. "Right Mam. I will sort all the solicitors bills out for you, so don't worry. Anyway,what happened" asked Williams. " Well son, what are those microwave meals all about? I told the nice officer I would go in there and sort the meals out for them. You can't beat fresh cooked food. Gotta love her thought Williams. " Mam, when are you in court ?" he asked. "Oh next month. On the sixteenth I think". "Right" said Williams . " I'll get off now". Williams was on his way to his car when he heard his phone ringing. Jonno's name came up on the screen. " Alright Jonno. How are you? " "Yeah sound mate." replied Jonno " I heard Pope stitched you up and you got arrested for it!" Williams was gob smacked. " Really? " shrieked Williams. "Look I'm at my Mam's. I will phone you in about twenty minutes" ....

Chapter 9-Choices

"Hello Jonno. It's me, Williams"

"Yeah I can see that" said Jonno, with a hint of sarcasm.

"Right. What have you heard mate?" Williams could barely contain his curiosity.

"Well. Someone heard that girl,Shazza talking how Pope had found a letter you sent to her saying you had that painting off " replied Jonno

"And ?" said Williams

"Well, he phoned his mates in the constabulary, to get you back for stitching him up" replied Jonno.

"Oh. he fucking did,did he? spat Williams

"Yeah mate,sorry to be the one to tell ya " said Jonno genuinely.

"Right Jonno. Go and see Shazza and tell her Williams wants to know what side of the fence she's on. Send your Scott in as well to. I ain't having this. As well she should know "

"Yeah right mate no problem" replied Jonno, before adding "Oh ,and I heard they are getting married as well "

"Oh really ?" Williams said menacingly.

Williams then went back to the museum to get his thoughts together and to see how the job was getting on. It was now he was beginning to realise that his windfall was slowly slipping through his fingers . Less than nine months ago he had half a million pounds ,now he was down to his last one hundred thousand and it really was going down fast. The next payment was due for the work the following week ,so even what he had left was not going to be enough to pay for the court case and the museum. He had to make a choice. Finish the work or make sure his Mam got the best solicitors money could buy ……. There was no choice and as much as he loved the museum as a kid and wanted everyone to share in the joys he had there , his Mam would always come first. He phoned the solicitor and said "Mike. I don't care what it costs, you just have to get my Mam off. "Don't worry" said Mike. "We will do our best and worse case scenario she will only get twelve months" Williams was horrified. "Twelve months? Twelve months would kill her mate! " . Mike tried to be reassuring. "Don't worry Si,. I will do my best" he said to Williams. For the first time in his life, Williams didn't know what to do for the best. The second payment for the work went out of the bank as agreed and the work was going great..unlike Williams' finances ,that he had pounded , over the last few months. In fact after the solicitors bills there would be nothing left. little did everyone know that Williams was on the verge of being potless .   ;

Chapter 10-Five minutes of fame

After several visits from his solicitor and what seemed to be hundreds of letters , Williams new the bill was going to be very large and would really clean him out. The day of the trial arrived and the Crown Court was full to the brim with reporters. They were all wanting to find out how a seventy two year old woman could be the mastermind behind the theft of one of Salford's finest paintings all those years ago. Mrs Williams arrived dressed in a new blouse she had just that morning, received from QVC , the shopping channel. It was a good job really, as the media scrummage was truly unbelievable. Camera crews from as far away as China had even turned up to find the truth behind the story. The trial started with the jury being sworn in. The prosecution then started to ask Mrs Williams how she came about the painting. The courtroom was in tears of laughter when she replied. "I got it off mike the pot man. The one with the dangly earring. Everybody knows him, don't they? It's like I told that kind officer in the station Why should I lie?" The prosecution lawyer, getting somewhat frustrated, said " Mrs Williams, your son has sold a painting worth half a million pounds and you are saying you bought it from a flea market?"
"I am. I was with Sandra Pilkington, I think she will be giving evidence in a minute." It was at this point in the proceedings that the judge summoned the defence and the prosecution into his chambers. After ten long minutes of empty silence in the court ,the judge returned. He directed his following comments to the prosecution. " So,you have a letter from a former policeman saying that Mrs Williams is the criminal genius behind the robbery and that is the basis of the arrest of this pensioner? " The judge looked furious. "How on God's earth has this case got into my courtroom. It is within my powers to throw this case out before we are made to look even more foolish. I dismiss the jury and you ,Mrs Williams are free to leave this court with your good name still intact. The courtroom erupted in cheers and Mrs Williams was led from the dock with her arms in the air shouting " Justice has been served! " to the waiting reporters outside the court. William's solicitor read them a brief statement concluding with "This case has not only been a waste of taxpayers money but it has also been a waste of this innocent lady's time and her very good name".
Williams thought to himself "Yeah, and the rest of my money."

Williams went back to his Mum's with the Blue Rinse Mafia. When they were all at home, every single TV, in every single house in Mrs Williams' road was on. The Mafia's members were eagerly watching the local news for a glimpse of themselves. Funny how on the day of Mrs Williams' arrest the Blue Rinse Mafia looked like they could do with a well needed makeover, yet on the day of her release they were all decked in twin sets. One or two of them had even dug the fake furs out of their wardrobes. The local hairdressers, Scissorhands, on Orient Road, had ran out of perming lotion and the staff had worked their fingers to the bone. The last time they had used that much perming lotion was in 1998 for the grand opening of the Gala Bingo hall. It had been their 15 minutes of fame and they had well and truly pushed the boat out!

Williams and his mum sat down after Mrs Williams had made her son a brew.

"I'm glad it's all gone okay, Mum", said Williams.

"Do me a favour, son. Stop getting involved in all these hair brained schemes. You're 48 years old. You're not going to see Zack and Ella grow up the way you're going", Mrs Williams replied.

"Yea, I'm going to give it up. I'm sick of it all. There's just one thing to sort out in Spain. I'll be away for a few days.", he added.

"I'm getting off, Mum. See ya, girls", Williams said cheerfully. He left the group of ladies nattering and preparing to watch themselves all over again on ITV+1.

"See you, love. Be careful", Mrs Williams answered. The Blue Rinse Mafia completely ignored him as 'plus one' had started.

Chapter 11-Spanish sausage

Williams boarded Flight AZ 134 to Malaga unbeknown to him that the day before, the same flight had been in uproar due to the raucous behaviour of Mrs Froggatt, Mrs Hedgehog, Mrs Wilcox, Miss Ditchburn, Mrs Ordish, Mrs Lawson and a couple of bricklayers from Milton Keynes. At one point during the flight, the pilot threatened to land the plane in Madrid and throw them all off his aircraft. It was only the fact that Mrs Wilcox had slipped him her phone number as she had boarded the plane that had stopped him. He was never one to look a gift horse in the mouth.

After three hours of turbulence, Williams landed in Malaga and after buying three bottles of Smirnoff, swiftly made his way to a waiting taxi. He was going to stay at his old friends' house where he had stayed on his last visit to Malaga. As he made his way to the Johnson Boys' house he was thinking that he was going to have a great time . At the same time, revenge was firmly on his mind.

He knocked on the door which was quickly answered by Aunty Pat.

"You're looking a bit pale, lad", she said as she looked at Williams standing there, suitcase in one hand and a duty free bag in the other.

" Nothing a few days in the sun won't sort out, Aunty Pat", he said as he gave her a hug and a kiss on the cheek.

He then walked into the lounge where he was met by Scott and Graham.

" Hiya, mate. See you made it", said Graham, obviously glad to see the arrival of his old friend.

" Wouldn't miss it, mate. After what that bastard's put my mum through" Williams said.

"We've done what you asked, mate", Scott said.

"How much do I how you, lads?", Williams asked the dad and lad ,

"This one's on us. The results are going to be amazing. We've never liked him either", Graham informed Williams.

Back at the bar the Salford girls had arrived. The party was in full swing and I just knew that everything was going to be perfect. I was going to have the perfect wedding. Drinks were flowing and being consumed at an alarmingly fast rate. The karaoke was being abused by Mrs Hedgehog, Mrs Lawson and Mrs Ordish who, for some reason, thought they were Salford's answer to The Three Degrees. Mrs Ordish was taking things so seriously that she even pushed a little child out of the way when an Elvis song came on the screen. She never even batted an eyelid when the kid burst into floods of tears. Mrs Ditchburn and Mrs Wilcox were more interested in two builders from Barnsley, Dave and Pete, than they were in belting a good tune out. Frogatt meanwhile was downing jug after jug of Sangria complaining that it wasn't strong enough and it tasted more like Vimto. Despite her complaints that it wasn't strong enough she was almost comatose. Jonathon spotted Wilcox and Ditchburn sneaking out, quickly followed by the Barnsley Builders. The next morning, Jackie Frogatt came into the bar bright as a button, as if she hadn't had a drink. Five hours earlier I was on the verge of getting an ambulance to take her to the hospital. I reminded the Three Degrees about what they had been up to and they couldn't have cared less. "What goes on in Spain stays in Spain" they piped up in unison. I was beginning to dread what would happen next. With these girls anything was possible. As they left the bar for the day they told me they would be going shopping for some presents for their families and to get new frocks for the wedding. Only because they knew there would be a few of Jonathon's old friends there. They didn't want to miss a chance of some more action , especially Ditchburn who had a fetish for men in uniforms.

The girls said "Bye" and they'd be back later for my Hen Do .I was questioning my judgement about inviting them but I smiled and said "see you later".

The girls left and made their way to Malaga's answer to Hollywood Boulevard. The first shop they went into a designer perfume shop and Mrs Hedgehog was soon talking to the customer assistant in her best 'Spanglish'. She was using the age old Salford ploy of keeping the shop assistant distracted while the other girls were filling their bags to the brim with the shop's contents. The girls didn't believe in buying duty free when you could get it free . They left the shop with at least thousand Euros worth of perfume and not one of them had opened their purses.

After leaving the shop they went to the nearest bar and quickly ordered the first round of drinks:

" Six San Miguels and six shots, please" said Mrs Ordish before asking the barman what time the karaoke started.

"Karaoke start in one hour" said the barman in a very sexy Latino voice. Dithburn had already caught sight of a rather delicious looking Spaniard sat in the corner. She turned to Hedgehog and informed her

" I'll be having a bit of that later!"

Ditchburn wasn't interested in the possibility of being shown some of the local sights by one of the Malaguenos. Oh, no. She was more interested in the bulge she had spotted in his trousers, or rather the two bulges in his trousers. One being his wallet and the other being...well,

his....erm..salchichon (sausage, for the non Spanish speakers).

Five rounds of drinks later the girls were begging the barman to start the karaoke early. He obliged and started to plug all the equipment into the mains. No sooner had he asked did anyone want to start the proceedings off than the girls surrounded the barman and snatched the microphone out of his hands. They looked at the song list and after surveying the list Ordish said:

" I don't believe it!. They haven't got it. We're just gonna have to sing it without the music".

I don't think the locals had witnessed anything quite like it before as they listened to the group of inebriated women singing 'We're having a gangbang we're having a ball" with actions to accompany every line. The locals were probably never going to see anything like it again. Wilcox and Ordish were just about as drunk as anyone could get and still be conscious. If they had been men they would probably have been kicked out of the bar. They made Vinegar Vera and Sticky Vicky look like two high class socialites. You'd think that after their marathon drinking session they would want to just go back to their hotel and sleep wouldn't you? No, the women embarked on another shopping spree. However, the first shop assistant they encountered could not understand a word they were saying. As Ordish tried to act as the decoy for her pilfering friends, the assistant was trying hard to distinguish where her customer was from. She wasn't sure if she was Welsh, Scottish, English or Russian. She could hardly string two words together that made any sense. That is apart from the two Spanish words that Ordish knew. Mas and cerveza. Though God knows why they would teach you how to say " more beers" in school. Once again, the girls left the shop with their bags full and there purses no lighter as their shopping spree had cost exactly nothing. Having acquired what they needed, they then headed back to there hotel to get changed for the night ahead.

They arrived thirty minutes later at my bar ,where the champagne was already on ice. I just knew it was going to be one of those nights, and in the morning I was to marry the man of my dreams. Lawson pulled out all the usual hen do gear ,which meant I had to walk round wearing an L plate. I also had a list of things I had to do. Put it this way, I drew the line at several of the things on the list. Hedgehog proudly said she had completed them all on her hen do. Ditchburn said she would complete the ones I couldn't . As the night grew on , I found myself a little bit torn .Not because of the wedding , that, I was sure about. It was because I could see how much my friends had that zest for life. They reminded me of Williams. They knew life was for living and boy did they live it. Later on the girls and I parted company as I had to be at my best for the morning. Besides,they had earlier in the day arranged to meet some locals. After saying our goodnights, I walked into my bar. I knew this time I wasn't going to leave my intended stood at the altar.

The girls meanwhile headed back to the bar where they had earlier brought the house down with their singing exploits. Ditchburn made a beeline for Senor Bulging Pants. He knew his luck was going in. Hedgehog turned to Froggat and said " What's up with you mate?" Froggat was not impressed at all "I will tell you what's up with me. I ain't being touched by any Spanish slime ball. I am going elsewhere". With this she left on her own and made her way into the less busy side of village. To her utter amazement, who was the first person bumped in to? It was Williams! He stood there as bold as brass with his two mates, the Jonno boys "Froggie! how are you mate?" , screamed Williams. Froggie was buzzing she was seeing a long lost friend for the first time in twenty years . "Will. How are you? and give us a kiss ". "No problem mate" said Williams with a cheesy grin. Williams lips met with Froggat's and they kissed tenderly. Foggier nearly melted on the spot .
" What you doing here Williams?" she asked . "Oh mate, it's a long story but we've got plenty of time so I will tell you. What you having to drink mate?" "Oh" said Froggy still reeling from the kiss "I will have a brandy and coke". Displaying his most charming smile, Williams said " You know what they say that does don't you ?" Froggat laughed "Yeah I do mate." Well go on then tell me." Williams told his story ." That ex plod Shazza is marrying set my Mam up. She nearly got sent down. Cost me a right few

quid to sort it all out. Anyway, now its payback time and I am going to buzz off them trust me. Did you know she robbed thirty grand of mine and bought that bar with Pope? " Froggat was gob smacked. "No I didn't "

"Yeah cheeky bitch. Then he phones his mates and tries to get my Mam sent down. Well they are going to get a shock in the morning I can tell you!." "Why? What you got lined up for them?" Williams smirked. " Just wait and see. They ain't taking the piss out of me and getting away with it I can tell you"

"Does anyone know you're here? asked Froggat.

"No, but they will tomorrow I can tell you. So don't say anything to anyone. Who you here with?"

"The old gang .Lawson , Ordish ,Wilcox ,Hedgehog and Ditchburn"

"God, she will go anywhere for a piss up that Ditchburn" said Williams, not really surprised.

"Yes, they were all with some spicks ,so I left them , I can't stand all that pretty English woman bollocks. So fake".

"Good girl Froggie you ain't changed. You with me all night then? Williams asked with a knowing look.

"Oh yes mate and make sure it is all night" replied Froggat.

Meanwhile, back at the bar Ditchburn was leaving with the Spanish waiter. He would be gutted in the morning as he would be completely empty and his wallet would be gone. The rest of the girls were singing and falling all over the place. Real classy.

I was woken up on my wedding morning at twenty past four with the girls being thrown out of their hotel , and banging on my door. There was no sign of Froggat ,who had been having the time of her life with Williams. She arrived twenty minutes later with the biggest smile on her face. The girls were puzzled and wanted to know why she looked like the cat who'd got the cream.

"Where have you been, Mrs?" asked Ordish, eager for the answer.

"Heaven, girls. Heaven", Froggat replied and when asked for more details she said:

" All I'll say is don't be surprised if he turns up today". And that was all she would say on the matter.

With that they made their way to the kitchen and between them ate a week's worth of food shopping.

Chapter 12-Payback Time

Mrs Frogatt was left in the kitchen to tidy up what resembled a bomb site. The rest of the crew had gone to the guest bedroom upstairs to get themselves ready for the afternoon nuptials. Frogatt was still a little bit worse for wear as she attempted to wash the breakfast pots that everyone had left that morning. Worried that she may be the last person in the lengthy queue for the bathroom she hastily switched all the appliances off and made her way upstairs.

 Upstairs it was bedlam. There was hardly room to swing a cat as it was but with the place full of women fighting over one mirror and two plug sockets it was hardly the most relaxed build up to my wedding day. Why the girls were bothering looking their finest for a congregation that was going to consist mainly of members of the GMP I didn't know. The force had probably seen them at their worst in the mug shots down at Salford cop shop.

Time was moving on I realised it was about time for the hairdresser to arrive. She was a local girl that I had used a few times and considering she couldn't understand a word I was saying, she seemed to know exactly what I wanted doing. I was in for the first shock of the day.

I rang her number and she promptly answered. As she said hello I expected to hear the noise of traffic as she drove to the bar but all I could hear was women chattering in the background.

"Are you on the way Maria?" I asked. "It's getting late".

" Oh, hello", she said in her broken English. " What's wrong Sharon? I not do hair today. You cancel last week. You tell me you not marry him because he a pig and bastard ".

I dropped the phone in complete shock. What was I going to do? I didn't even stop to question what could have happened for her to think that I had cancelled. All I could think about was the fact that my hair was a mess and there was no time to get someone else to do it.

After telling the girls what had happened Mrs Lawson stepped in and said: " I did 6 months at De La Salle college doing hair and beauty. Was a right bloody walk going to Weaste Lane everyday. I was knackered by the time I got there. Had to have a brew and a fag before I even thought about doing anybody's perm and set ".

"When did you do that?" asked Mrs Ditchburn.

"1987" , Mrs Lawson replied.

" Oh, for fuck's sake", I muttered under my breath. I really did not want to look like a cross between Pete Burns and a backing singer for Spandau Ballet but beggars can't be choosers so I said "OK "and very quickly washed my hair. I sat down and waited for Mrs L to do her worst.

At the end of an agonising hour the end result wasn't too bad at all. I think it was more good luck than down to her having done a course nearly thirty years ago. I thanked her then made my way upstairs to put the dress on. It had been hung in the wardrobe for months and now I was finally going to wear it.

I was just about to step into the dress when I heard the voice of Mrs Hedghog shout

" Where are you getting your flowers from, Sharon?"

" Oh, a little florist two streets away. Actually will you ring them and ask what time they are delivering them please? The number is on the cork board in the kitchen. Thanks" I said getting a little bit anxious as time was passing by.

Two minutes later shock number two was delivered as Mrs Hedgehog shouted to me:

"Sharon, I don't know how to tell you this but the florist said you cancelled your order last week on the grounds that the man you were going to marry was a pig and a bastard and a son of a bitch. Sharon, what are you going to do? "

This was not going to plan. I had thought about this day for months. Well, years actually. Not necessarily my wedding to Jonathan but my wedding to anyone. The day I was supposed to marry Williams just didn't feel right. It wouldn't have been for the right reasons but this time it was.

"Don't worry, Sharon. The fact you're getting married is what matters", said Mrs O. At this point I was wondering what else could go wrong. I was soon to find out as I rang the confectioner.

I asked what time they would deliver the cake as we were all about to leave for the chapel very soon. The reply was the final straw.

" You cancel order last week. You not remember? You say 'Is all off. I not marry that pig, bastard, son of a bitch, snake if he the last man on earth"

The confectioners broken English words faded as I put the phone down and sat dumbstruck. There was something not quite right. It didn't take an Inspector Morse to suss that one out.

I decided that all this was not going to ruin the day even if I was starting to get a little bit upset.

The time had arrived for the cars to arrive. Suddenly I realised they weren't going to come. Rather than phone to see where they were, I couldn't face going through the whole 'pig, bastard, son of a bitch, snake ' routine again, I decided to order two taxis to take us to the chapel. It was when I was sat in the back of the taxi and I approached the chapel that I saw Jonathan and all our guests stood outside that I realised that everything that could possibly go wrong was going wrong.

I stepped out of the car and walked over to Jonathan and asked him what was happening. He told me that the chapel was shut for a week and there was nothing that they could do about it. The vicar, who was stood next to Jonathan stepped forward and said:

" In the eyes of God I can marry you anywhere. Right here if you would like", opening up his arms and gesturing towards the market place not 100 yards away.

Jonathan and myself immediately agreed. We informed our guests what was going to happen and asked them to take their positions in the nearby market square. The congregation sorted themselves into two groups; my side and Jonathan's side.

Just then the vicar coughed for attention and began the ceremony. By saying:

" We are all here today with Jonathan Alan Pope and Sharon Hermione Imogen Thompson. They are about to enter into the binding contract that is marriage. Before they enter into that contract I have to ask is there anyone present that knows any reason why they shouldn't legally be husband and wife?"

At that moment Williams appeared to gasps of my so called friends who were all nudging each other. I thought I heard a wolf whistle but I couldn't be sure. All of a sudden the girls realised that GMP's finest weren't the best option there that day, it was Williams. My so called new mate Frogatt was grinning as Williams said the words:

" I do".

He then launched into a verbal barrage aimed at the both of us. He started with Jonathan, saying

" You call yourself a man? Trying to set up a 72 year old woman. You're not a man in my eyes. You shit. Not only did your plan backfire and it was laughed out of court. You deserve everything that is coming your way. It was then that Jonathan's ex colleague said:

" I'm going to have you for this!".

"What? Like I've had your missus?. I'd like to say it was good too but I'd be lying" said Williams with venom in every word he uttered.

"There's nothing you or your la-de-dah mates can do over here. So if I were you lot I'd take my advice and keep your mouths shut".

I thought he was going to leave it at that but he continued by pointing his finger at me and said:

" And as for you. Rob me out of thirty grand would you? Choose to go on his side of the fence would you? Well I hope it's all worth it! Did you get your hair done? Oh, and the flowers and the cake and the church? Pig, bastard. Son of a bitch snake. Ring any bells. Oh and one last thing. The lovely vicar is Scott Dixon the tattooist from Candy Skull tattoo shop in Swinton. He spends his spare time as an amateur actor at St Luke's amateur dramatic society on Liverpool Street. Isn't that right Scott?"

"Yes, Williams" , the vicar replied.

No sooner had the impostor confirmed his true identity, there was an explosion coming from the vicinity of my bar. Life couldn't get much worse. Williams looked us both in the eye, smirked and said:

" Payback".

Blowing the bar up was just an added bonus to Williams. The icing on the non existent cake you might say. Was it a coincidence that Williams had spent the night with Mrs Frogatt , who it seemed had left one of the gas rings on? I was in a state of shock. Everything we had worked for was gone. The biggest day of my life ruined by the man I once loved so much. Jonathon and I had put everything into that bar and now we had nothing left but each other ,

Williams walked away and I never saw him again. Nor did I ever want to.

Chapter 13-On the radio

Williams arrived back at Manchester airport ,with just enough money to see him through the week. However, he had sorted out what he needed to do. Now, he had to find the money to pay the builders. He also had a radio interview to do about the museum the following day. His head really was in bits. He sat outside the museum with twenty stirling and a bottle of vodka , not knowing which way to turn (unlike the bottle top which he soon cracked open). He woke early the next morning and thought It better to get a shower before going to the radio station. He went to his Mam's ,he had a quick shower and headed off to the radio station. He was met by the studio manager Sufiya . "Morning simon" she said. Joe is in there waiting for you ,

Williams open the door and shook Joe Barnwell's hand.

"Hello Simon. Welcome to the Joe Barnwell show, Something Old Something New. Simon is here to tell us the story of him turning something old into something new"

"Thanks Joe. Pleasure to be here"

"We'll be chatting to Simon straight after this. There's A Light by The Smiths"

"Right Simon, its great what you have done. What has gave you the inspiration?" asked Joe.

"Well Joe, I got a bit sick and tired of seeing Salford landmarks ripped down before my eyes. Seedley school. Tootal Road school. Salford rugby ground. And what's there now? Nothing but waste land. Its criminal what is happening to our great city. It just isn't right and the council have got so much to answer for"replied Williams .

"I couldn't agree with you more" said Joe

"Anyway, I saw some school kids visiting the museum on the Crescent and the bus they were in nearly had a crash. Really shook me up. So, I came up with this idea. Get the Buile Hill Museum back to its former glory,give it back to Salford council . Then, get them to sell the building they are using on the Crescent to the university and move everything to Buile Hill Park. It's much safer there for the kids. No roads to cross. It makes more sense to use this great building. The money they get for selling the Crescent site can go to the upkeep" said Williams

"I couldn't agree with you more, Simon. Seems like you have really thought this through" said Joe

"Yeah mate. I had to because nobody else is. Are they? The people we gave our vote to. It seems to me like they are just in it for the money" said Williams

" So, how did you get to find out about the museum?" asked Joe .

Williams smiled. "Well mate, funny really. I asked Hazel Mears about a year ago who owned it. She got back in touch after a few weeks saying the council owned it. I had forgotten all about it until I saw her at my lads parents evening. She said there were a few grants available and it didn't cost a lot of money to be honest. The only real problem was the dry rot, which I didn't allow for in my calculations.

Sorting that cost me nearly as much as the building!" Williams continued.

"Great. Well I for one am proud of what you have done and I only wish there were more like you in this city" exclaimed Joe.

Williams' reply was instant. "There are! There's thousands like me Joe. That's what makes this city great"

Nodding in agreement, Joe replied "Yes Simon it is. So full of life, and most of us live it to the full.

"Look Joe. I've got something to tell you" said Williams

Over the introduction to Our House by Madness, Joe announced that Williams' confession would be right after the song.

As the song faded, Joe continued.

"OK Simon. You said you had something to tell us?"

"Yes Joe, I do. I don't quite know how to say this but here goes"

Williams took a deep breath and started to pour his heart out.

" You know I sold the painting and got half a million?" Williams said to Joe, who was all ears.

"Yes, I think everyone in Salford knows about it", said Joe.

"Well, I went a bit daft at first to be honest, Joe" Williams continued.

"Spending money on clothes, women and a flash car. Then my mum was blatantly set up. I had to sort her solicitor's bills out. I had to get her the best, She's my Mam. I've really got nothing left mate. Just the clothes I'm sat here in. I've still got to pay nine grand to the builders for their work. I still owe them that. I am so sorry that I've let the proud people of my home city down. I'm gutted".

Seconds after saying these last words, Williams broke down crying.

"Simon. Don't cry. At least you've had a go and you deserve some respect for that", said Joe.

"Yeah, but I've let everyone down", replied Williams with his head slumped forward clearly very upset.

Joe had planned his play list the day before his show and was unprepared for the poignancy of the track he was about to play. Williams looked about as low as a man could get when the first few bars of the song started. Inspiral Carpets singing 'This is how it feels to be lonely this how it feels to be small ..this is how it feels when your word means nothing at all'. They were not the words that Williams needed to hear. He felt as though the whole city was whispering and saying his name and for all the wrong reasons.

Joe let the track finish but seemed preoccupied. He was watching red lights flickering on and off on the screen in front of him.

" Simon, something appears to be happening here in the studio. The phone lines are lighting up like a Christmas tree. I have a call form a June Davidson in Seedley" said Joe.

The lady was put through to Williams who really wasn't prepared for what he was about to hear.

" Don't get upset, Simon. You can have a fiver out of my pension. Didn't you go to school with my daughter, Dawn?" asked the lady at the end of the phone.

" Thanks June" said Williams. "Yeah I did. Wasn't she quiet like me?" Williams asked.

"Not at mine, she isn't", said June.

" I really appreciate it " said Williams, wondering how on earth a fiver was going to help to dig himself out the gigantic hole that he was in. However, he didn't have enough time to think about it because Joe interrupted his thoughts saying:

" We have another call from an Adele Hart in Tyldesley", said Joe.

"Hi, Simon. I've just been listening. I'll give you ten quid. I think it's great what you have done. The only thing is you'll have to wait til Monday when I get my family allowance" the friendly voice at the end of the line said.

"Thank you" said Williams who was starting to feel a little overwhelmed by people's generosity. The red lights kept on flashing.

Joe was put through to another caller.

"It's that the local MP, Hazel Mears?"asked Joe.

"Yes, it is Joe. Now listen Simon. I've seen the work you've done there and I will give you a thousand pounds towards the amount you owe", she said.

"Thank you, Hazel", said Simon. Joe was listening intently to the conversation and couldn't resist chipping in.

" You might even be able to claim it back on your tax returns, love".

Joe and Williams looked at each other and Williams smiled for the first time in hours . Joe didn't have much time to say anything else before the next call was put through.

" We have a Paul Quinn of the Town Hall in Eccles on the line. What would you like to say to Simon, Paul?" asked Joe.

"I will give you the same as Hazel has just given you. You've spent more than 10 times that in my pub over the years pal", said the voice before adding, " I'll do a charity night for you as well to raise funds. You can have all the profits. From the door I mean, not the bar of course".

Williams was almost stunned into silence by what was happening. He just about managed to reply " I've always had a top time in there as well Quinny"

Joe was almost as shocked as Williams.

"What can I say? In the space of four phone calls we've had over two grand donated. Incredible. That's a great start".

Williams could barely contain his emotions." Yea, Joe. I'm overwhelmed and I really just don't know what to say" And still the lights continued flashing.

"We have a Joel Higgins from Hope on the line", said Joe, checking the clock and thinking he wasn't going to get off on time today. Joe wasn't really that bothered because this was turning into something that he had never witnessed before.

 The callers voice came through the headphones." I will give you a hundred pound. I love the work you've done for us; the people of Salford. I personally think you should stand for mayor. Your heart is in this city. That's what we need; someone who cares".

" I couldn't agree more", said Joe.

"Thank you for your kind words, Joel. I don't think I'm mayor material", said Williams in answer to the man's suggestion.

" Wow" said Joe. " I'll leave you to think about that one Simon, while we listen to 'I Can't Stand Losing You by The Police. While the rest of Salford was humming along to the song, Joe and Simon chatted.

"Right Simon. Can you stay with us for another hour? We're going through to the news" asked Joe

"Yeah. Course I can Joe. I don't have any plans for the time being" answered Williams

"Great" said Joe. Salford City Radio will help get you this money"

The newsreader summed up the events of the day and handed back to Joe.

"Right listeners. We need six and a half grand. Can we do it? Of course we can. Pick up the phone and give as much or little as you like. Every penny really helps"

As if planned, Money Money Money by Abba was up next.

" Next up Simon we have another caller. Rose Briggs, from The Westwood Estate."

"Hiya love I ain't got any money to give but I will come and clean up for you on Monday. If that's OK" said Rose

"Oh yes. Of course" said Williams, hardly believing what he was hearing.

"Thank you Rose, that would be great and I look forward to seeing you"

Williams was not prepared for what came next. "Simon,we have just had a call from a director at PLD and he says just pay what you can afford now, and if you want your old job back, be in the yard on Monday!"

"Wow. I really don't believe what's happening. It's so surreal. The museum will be ready on Friday. I feel like screaming" shouted Williams.

Joe laughed out loud. "Well go on then don't let me stop you"

Williams let out an almighty "YESSSSS"

"Appropriately, the next track says it all" grinned Joe. " Congratulations"

 As soon as the track had finished playing. Another call. "Simon we have a call from an old workmate of yours. Andy Jordan in Burnley" said Joe.

 "Andy. What can I do for you mate?"

"Its more what I can do for you. I've just come into some money and me and the missus have decided to give the museum five grand. Said Andy form Burnley.

Williams' was smiling more than he'd ever smiled in his life. "That's an amazing gesture for a dingle mate".

" Ha ha. I'm proud to be a dingle" laughed Andy.

"Thanks so much mate". said Williams

Joe sat back in his chair. "Bet you're so made up Simon? I know I am"

" I .Just don't know what to say and I'm never lost for words! How I can thank the people of Salford enough?" asked Williams.

" The next track is a special one. Just for Simon and his Mam. It's Brian and Michael singing the Salford anthem, Matchstalk Men & Matchstalk Cats & Dogs"

As the familiar strains of the brass band faded out with the song, Joe wrapped up the show.

"Thanks for being on the show Simon and good luck you really deserve it mate"

"Joe. The pleasure really has been all mine mate. I can't thank you enough"said a very humbled Williams .They shook hands and Williams left the studio much happier than when he arrived.

Chapter 14-Back to work

Williams headed straight for one of his watering holes, The Inn of Good Hope. At the bar, he bumped into his old friend Stuart 'Homo' Holmes. Williams greeted his old friend. "Alright mate? Hows thing's? I ain't seen you in ages"

"Am great, mate" answered Homo. " I heard you on the radio before you sounded alright. Did you really cry?"

"Yeah mate. I was getting a bit depressed. Everything always seems to go tits up for me no matter how hard I try" said Williams.

" I don't know why your being like that .Stop being a mard arse will you?" said Homo.

"Listen mate. Less than 9 months ago I had half a million quid. Now what have I got? Nothing" Williams was feeling a bit sorry for himself.

"You got your mates and that's all you need" said Homo.

"Yeah you're right" replied Williams. With this, they sat down and started to reminisce about the old times.

Homo laughed "Remember when we went up town that night and you put my dad's pants on and they were too short?"

Williams agreed "Yeah it was funny that mate"

Homo continued "Oh and do you remember when that tramp picked our pockets?

"Yeah. Only that wasn't funny "scowled Williams. "That was my last fiver. Come to think of it and I ain't got much more now mate."

"Are you really that skint? " asked homo.

"Yes mate. Spent the lot. At least I can sleep at night. I had a great nine months spending it all though " said Williams before adding "Look mate can you do us a favour? I need a suit for Friday. There is a big opening do at the museum. The mayor is gonna be there. Ryan Giggs , Adrian Morley. All the big wigs from Salford. I think that the painter Harold Riley is going to be there" said Williams, feeling quite proud.

"Yeah. Of course I can,not a problem. What waist are you?

" I am a thirty two"

"Well I better give you a belt as well because I am a thirty four" said Homo

"Cheers Homo"

"Where you going later? Asked Homo. Looks like I am back at my Mam's for a few nights till I get sorted.".

"Best steak for a tenner a week" laughed Homo.

"Oh yes. Happy days eh mate? I ain't looking forward to work on Monday though"said Williams.

"Why mate?" asked Homo.

" To be honest mate, I've been taking the piss on that museum job and I know they will get their own back"

"You'll just have to see how it goes, mate" said Homo.

Williams met back in the yard on Monday and he wasn't wrong. They had him working all day long on a site in Eccles, on the Ellesmere Park estate. He was knackered by the time he got home and fell fast asleep. Only waking up when it was time for work again. Once again,they had him doing everything. Funnily enough though, Williams always found time for a cup of tea. Williams was cleaning up outside a house and a young mum said to him "You fancy a brew love?"

"Oh yes please" said Williams, spitting feathers "I haven't had a brew all day "

"Well you better come in then and get a warm"

Williams was very grateful " Cheers love I'm freezing".With this she let him in. Williams introduced himself. " Hi I'm Simon"

"Yes, I have seen you picture in the paper. You're the one who sorted the museum out aren't you? I'm Jackie. Jackie Royle" Williams thought the formal introduction was a bit strange. He only wanted a brew and a warm. Jackie had more than a cup of tea on her mind and invited Williams round later that night when the kids were in bed. Williams wasn't tired at all that night, strangely enough. At half ten on the dot, Williams called round to Jackie's and got more than a cup of tea this time. Deed done, Williams was back home half an hour later. His life was complicated enough, so when she messaged and called him later, he just didn't answer the phone or her texts. This, understandably made Jackie very angry. So angry in fact that she put in a complaint against Williams. He was called into the office on the Thursday night. The two company directors quizzed him about what had happened. Bold as brass, Williams explained it the best way he could. "Well, it's like being offered a brew. If I'm offered one I am going to have it. Sugar, biscuits and all. Never look a gift horse, mate" Williams does have quite a unique way with words. The directors looked at one another, shook their heads and said "Look Williams, you've only been back four days and already you're causing chaos. We have to be seen to do something about it.

We've decided you have to be moved to another site." Williams was overjoyed as the work on that site was hard graft. The new one might be a little easier. Williams, once again landing on his feet turned to leave the office. He looked back over his shoulder and said "Oh, by the way I wont be in tomorrow I am at the museum.

"Yes, yes we know. So are we. We did the work, remember? " With that Williams left the office feeling very excited abut his big day.

Chapter 15-Outburst

Williams woke early in the morning as he was all excited about his big day. His youngest son, Sam was even more excited as he would be meeting Ryan Giggs. Sam had made sure all his mates at Light Oaks School knew. He had a pocket full of match attack cards and he would make sure that Giggsy signed them.

Williams arrived at the museum just in time for the mayor to give his speech. Williams looked around the huge crowd that had gathered and spotted all of his family. He was bursting with pride. Little Sam made a bee line for Giggs and was tugging at his pants to get his attention. Giggsy signed the cards and made Sam's day. In fact probably his year!! The mayor started his speech. " It gives me great pleasure to be here today to open this fine old building . We at the council have worked very hard to get it open and we will continue to do our very best for the people of Salford. Williams wasn't quite sure what he was going on about. He stepped up to the platform where the mayor was standing. "Psst. Is it OK if I say a few words?" whispered Williams. The mayor looked quite put out and hissed " if you must."

Williams then said the words that were going to make a lot of people sit up and start taking notice of him. "You Mr Mayor and your friends on the council have done nothing for this museum or this park. In fact,come to think of it you've done nothing for the people of Salford either. This city has been on a downward spiral for years. You have sold all the council houses making it impossible to get one, even if you're from Salford. You have transferred all the houses to City West or Salix homes . Losing even more assets. You have cut the collection of bins to once a fortnight instead of weekly. You are tearing the heart out of the city. Local landmarks like Salford Rugby Ground , Seedley School , Tootal Road School all gone, sold out from under us, and replaced by what? I will tell you what. Wasteland. That's what. You have destroyed our transport system this city by selling the bus routes to GMPTE. Well I for one, ain't having it no more, which is why I put most of my money into this. You, Mr Mayor can stick your fancy opening day right up your arse. You and your council cronies should hang your heads in shame. I bet not a single one of you money grabbing free loaders actually live in this city" Williams was raging. He threw the microphone at the mayor and stormed off the platform. The crowd stood and stared open mouthed. The TV, press and radio had a massive story that they couldn't have made up. Williams got his kids together and they headed home, taking their usual route down Chaseley Road and across the De La Salle playing fields. What should have been a happy day for Williams had left him fuming.

The following day, the headlines in the local paper ,The Salford City Reporter, were

Museum's saviour in council outburst

Williams' phone was ringing early the following morning. It was Amanda, Williams' daughter.

" I see you're in the Reporter again, Dad".

"Are there any pictures?" asked Williams.

"Yea" replied Amanda before adding "The suit looks a bit baggy though".

" I borrowed it from Homo. That's why it's a bit baggy", Williams told her.

"Bring us a copy round then, love. I could do with laugh", he said.

"Oh, Dad", said Amanda " I almost forgot. Can you have Zac and Ella tonight? You'll be alright. Zac goes to bed at 8 and Ella sleeps right through after her bottle at half 7. It will be a doddle for you. We'll drop them off at 7 and pick them up at 12", said Amanda. She gave Williams very little option other than to say "Yes. OK"

As the day wore on Williams was quite looking forward to having his grandkids for the evening. The day passed quickly and before he knew it, they were knocking on the front door. Little Zac was so pleased to see his granddad that he was jumping up and climbing all over him. Ella was just as pleased to see her granddad and was smiling at him showing off her angelic blue eyes. They would get whatever they wanted off Williams. They were his pride and joy. However,he had never babysat them for this long before, so he was a little bit anxious to say the least.

 For the first hour it was going perfectly. Zac was telling Williams all about his favourite football team, Manchester United, and Williams was listening intently. The little boy said to his granddad:

" Granddad, can I see your football programmes please?".

" Yea, I'll go and get them. Be a good lad while I go and find them. Don't wake Ella up" added Williams.

Williams found the programmes after a few minutes and went back downstairs to find that Ella had been covered in the latest edition of the Salford Reporter from head to toe.

"What have you done, Zac?", asked Williams.

"I've made our Ella a little tent to keep her warm" said Zac. Williams was horrified at the sight of sheets of newspaper strewn over Ella's carrycot and even more sheets all over the house.

Williams gave Zac the programmes to look at while he started the job of picking all the newspapers up.

It was while Williams was picking the last of the newspapers and ripping them up in frustration that Zac said to his granddad:

" Here you are Granddad. Here's some more" Zac passed Williams his most treasured programme from the 1966 World Cup Final. It was in shreds. Williams was distraught. He did not know which way to turn. So, in desperation he turned to Facebook and asked for help. His status read: *Looking after my 2 grandkids. Can anyone help me please?*

Is was then that his old friend, Rose Stubbs, replied to his request for help. *'Simon, I'll be round in five minutes'* read the post.

Thank God for that, thought Williams. I might be able to watch the nine o'clock film if she hurries up.

Rose came round and greeted Williams with a kiss. Within minutes of arriving Rose started to tidy up and even responded to Williams' request that she change Ella's nappy. (Williams considered this to be a woman's job) .

Williams and Zac went upstairs for a wrestling match to find out who would be WWF champion of Salford. It was only when Rose shouted up for them to stop because she thought the bed was going to fall through the ceiling that Williams decided it was Zac's bedtime. Williams told Zac a story about how he had been heavyweight boxing champion of India when he was in the army. His little grandson went to sleep 'made up' as we say in Salford. Both grandkids were fast asleep and now it was time for Williams to have some fun.

Williams sat on the setee next to Rose and they settled down to watch the film. Williams poured himself a very large vodka as he needed to relax. Rose had a small glass of wine as she was driving and Williams only had little glasses (unless it was for the vodka). After his third drink and the bottle being almost empty, Williams nodded off. Rose felt a little bit annoyed as Williams seemed to ignore her for the vodka. She should have known better. It was time for her to leave.

Five minutes after Rose had left ,Amanda and Gaz knocked on the door, waking Williams up. He let them in and said "They have been no trouble what so ever. "They can stay again any time"

Chapter 16-The Salford wedding of the year

Time had flown for Williams over the following few weeks as so much had happened in his life. It seemed to pass at one hundred miles an hour. It seemed that one minute he was on his uppers. Next minute he was back down there and looking for something to eat from the pickings in his fridge. In his own mind though, he knew he had done the right thing with the museum. He might not have a pot to piss in but he had his friends and he knew things would change for the better. One of his good friends Phil Coussins was getting married to the lovely Laura and they had invited Williams to the wedding. To Williams, this was going to be an eye –opener. He had never ever seen so many people crammed into St Luke's Church on Liverpool St. It seemed to him that anyone who was anybody in Salford was there . The only difference to his wedding and the wedding of Charles and Diana was there were more people at Phil's. Oh, and Laura had a better dress than Diana. It was probably the Salford wedding of the year. The only thing wrong with the day was that Williams didn't have a date. Only a few months earlier, Williams could have had his pick of dates. It's amazing what a few quid can do. Well the wedding went without any hitches and a great day was had by all. It has been said that the celebrations went on in some houses down Weaste for a good few weeks. Far be it on me to comment on that. All I will say is look on Facebook for the pictures. They are there under 'Salford Wedding of the Year 2013'. Williams left the wedding early as it was a Friday and he had to pick his kids up. He was gutted because his ex missus, Tina, had talked her way into an invite. This left Williams to collect the kids. Fortunately for him,it just so happened that Rose had asked him if he fancied a date that night. She had tickets for the circus. What she didn't expect was Williams to turn up with his three kids. When Williams turned up, Rose's face was a picture. I don't think she was expecting the entire family!! As we know, that's Williams for you. Never one to do the normal thing, like cancel. He was glad he didn't as his kids had a fantastic time watching all the performers .Sam loved it and is still talks about it now. Especially the bit when he got to ride on an elephant. To this day he is convinced he is Indiana Jones. Williams smiled at the thought of his youngest running away to join the circus one day to be a lion tamer or a tightrope walker. The youngest member of the Williams brood really did have a great time. Rose also had a great time, laughing and sharing jokes with Williams all night. It was only when he had to leave Rose that he was sad. Williams wanted the joy of the night to last forever. Unfortunately, that was the last time he was to ever see Rose. Once again, Williams' life was about to change.

Williams went back in work the following morning. Another hard days graft getting the slates down and back on the wagon. The day seemed to go quickly. " Hey Williams" said Binnsy " Did you hear that, on the news" "Did I hear what on the news?" asked Williams.

"You're never going to believe this, mate but the mayor has had a heart attack"

" You're joking. I hope it wasn't anything to do with me throwing that microphone at him" smirked Williams.

" They said he has to stand down cos of the stress with the job and they are looking for a new mayor" said Binnsy

"Now there's a top job for someone. Do diddly shit and get a right packet" "Bit like you eh, Williams?" laughed Azza , only half joking.

Williams mocked "Oh listen to Azza now he has got a few airs on .Williams and Azza laughed out loud. Williams, always having to have the last word added. " Listen Azza. I got undies as old as you and some of the holes in them are nearly as old as you" they all laughed. Not five minutes later, Williams received a phone call from work . "Look Williams, we have been asked by the Salford City Reporter for your phone number. Should we give it to them?" asked the secretary. "No!!"said Williams "All they ever do is give me bad press and they keep using ugly shoots of me. If it was down to them, I would never ever get a bird , using them awful pictures" he said "I am surprised you ever get them anyway" replied the secretary.

"Yeah? How is your Mam?"said Williams "Tell her I was asking about her" meaning to hint that he could well be her Father. She wasn't impressed and cut Williams off, thinking she might just give them that phone number after all. "What was all that about ?"asked Binsy, puzzled.

"Dunno mate. The Salford City Reporter want my number for something." Azza looked quite excited " Hey,you might have won that season ticket that Koukash was giving away for a box at all the games."

" Could be. That would be good. I could go there. I don't think that my banning order applies to the rugby games , replied Williams. The rest of the day went by without incident. After work,Williams headed straight home to make his tea. As he got to the front door he heard a voice saying "Mr Williams?" Williams' first thought was "Oh shit. It's the TV licence man. He turned round and said "Yes that's me. What's up? "

"Nothing, Mr Williams. I am from the Salford City Reporter. Ho do you feel about standing for Mayor in the next elections in four weeks time?" asked the reporter. Williams looked puzzled and said " I got a job mate so that isn't going to happen. I would like to know what you're doing at my door though? How do you know where I live?

"I just looked on the council register, Mr Williams and it gave me your address".

"Oh really?" said Williams.

"Yes really" replied the reporter. " Anyone can access the records".

"Well, here's your story. it ain't going to happen. I can assure of that and you can quote me on that " said Williams. He stormed into his house and slammed the door behind him, leaving the reporter in no doubt there would be no more comments. Williams decided he needed a nice hot bath. While the tub was filling. his phone started ringing. He answered and on the other end was his Mam. She told him there had been a a bloke from the Manchester Evening News knocking at her door asking if he was standing for mayor. " No I ain't Mam. I don't know where all this is coming from. I was in work today and someone had been on to them asking for my number. I told them not to give it out. Then, I gets home from work and a fella was waiting outside the door, asking if I was going to run for Mayor. Me, a Mayor? What a joke. Someone is having a laugh."

Evidently not, as the the next morning, the local newspapers carried the headline...

New Mayor. Only 1 choice. The People's Choice. .. Williams.

Williams was in a state of shock as he went into the work. Binnsy wasted no time in saying "God, the papers are all full of you today aren't they mate ?"

" I know mate. All because I told them what I thought of them because the Mayor and his cronies were trying to get all the glory for something they hadn't done. It make you sick doesn't it mate? replied Williams.

"I know. They are a joke. You should give it a go and see what happens mate" Binnsy was serious.

"No chance mate, I ain't got a clue what to do" said Williams.

Binnsy laughed. "No. Neither do they do they. Just be yourself . I will vote for you and I will get Dianne to vote for you as well. Trotty will as well, won't you Trotty?"

"Yeah mate. Least I can do after you gave us that box at old Trafford" replied Trotty.

"Yeah. Go for it" chipped in young Azza you would be like a breath of fresh air ,my dad says , chirped young Azza. "You're just what that council needs. Someone with balls who will say no more cuts to the services"

"No. I don't think its for me" said Williams shaking his head. "I am just a labourer".

" I heard you get one hundred and forty thousand a year" winked Trotty.

"Really??" shrieked Williams.

"Yeah and a car and a gold chain. You tell them what to do ,they don't tell you. You can shout and moan as much as you want and get paid for it" added young Azza.

"You never know" said Binnsy "You might get in. Why don't you try?"

"Oh I don't know" said Williams, actually considering it for the first time. " I bet I wouldn't get any votes. The only ones I would get would be off you lot. That adds up to about ten. I'd look like a right ball and bat wouldn't I , with ten votes?"

"Hey. Look at this" said Azza, who had been looking at the morning paper. "Its that radio show you was on mate. It's only been nominated for a Sony award"

"I wonder if I get an invite?" said Williams. " I bet that would be a top piss up and you would see a few famous faces" Williams was brought back to reality by Trotty. " Right lads back to work. Oh, by the way. My missus has been on the phone and said the girls at her place will vote for you"

" Yeah. I bet they will"said Williams. " Get me their numbers then"

"Can't you be serious for once?" asked Trotty.

"I am being serious" said Williams. " So now, that would make all of twenty votes. The Monster Loony Party get more than that. Anyway .I ain't got five ton and I wouldn't have a clue what to say or do"

"Well. if you do decide to have a go, you need a campaign manager which is me" said Trotty. Williams thought he heard Binnsy mutter that Trotty couldn't manage a tank. At least that's what it sounded like. The trio went back to work. Williams, however, could not concentrate. All he could think about was the one hundred and forty grand a year wage for being Mayor. He worked out that on his current salary,it would take him eight years to get that. He was warming to the idea of being mayor.

Malcolm Liptrott, from the office approached Williams. "Listen Williams, the directors have been speaking and they will give you the five hundred pounds that you need to stand for Mayor"

Williams, as usual pushing his luck said "I would need two weeks off, with full pay of course to canvas for votes. Then, I might consider it". Liptrott went off to make a couple of phone calls and five minutes later he was back. " OK Williams, that's fine. You can have two weeks off from Monday as long as you mention the company. Oh, and all future council contracts for work in Salford go to us" Bribery was not something that Williams was going to stand for. This was exactly the kind of thing that Williams wanted to stamp out. He informed Liptrott that it wasn't going to happen like that. This turned out to be not one of his better decisions, as on the Friday he was told that the company had to let him go. Well, he had nothing to lose now. His mind was made up. He would have a go . Let the campaign trail begin.

Chapter 17- Expect the unexpected

Williams now needed five hundred pounds to stand for Mayor. He already had his campaign team in place. Trotty had seen to that. He explained to Williams how it would work. "What we have to do is get people in every part of the city to knock on every single door. We need feet on the street. We will have to sort out your polices. We need to get some leaflets and posters printed. I will get my mate, Dave Quinn and his mates to post them."

"Yeah mate. That sounds great but where we going to get the money to pay for all this?"asked Williams

"I ain't worked that bit out yet, mate but we will find a way. I ain't giving up over a grand" said Trotty, sounding like he was a man on a mission. You would have thought it was him standing for Mayor, not Williams. Trotty was relishing the idea of being Williams' manager. Williams was wondering how he could get the money together. Unusually for him, it had to be in an honest way as it wouldn't look to go if he was arrested just before the election. It was just then his daughter Amanda phoned him. " Hiya Dad. You know that old coal carving you gave us? Well, Gaz looked on the bottom and it was carved by that famous sculptor Steve Siddall from Walshaw. Seems its worth a right few quid. Gaz has put in on e-bay. It's got an hour to go and its already at six grand!"

"Wow. That's a result" said Williams.

" Yeah dad and we think its only right you get half as we know you ain't got anything" said Amanda.

"Aww. Thanks love. I can stand for Mayor now with that money" beamed Williams with pride. He had actually done some very good things in his life. Amanda was one of them.

" OK Dad. As soon as the bidding finishes I will phone you and let you know what it went for"said Amanda . Williams passed on the good news to Trotty. Trotty patted his good friend on the back and said " Look mate, everything is coming together. Things happen for reasons . This is your time". Trotty barely paused for a minute. He was on his work's phone which was taking a right bashing. He had been busy organising people from Weaste to Lower Broughton. Pendleton, Kersal ,Clifton, Eccles ,Little Hulton and even Irlam and Cadishead. Williams was even doing his bit as well, posing for pictures with babies. Visiting schools and nursing homes, Salford Royal. This time the Salford City Reporter hadn't let him down. His pictures were quite flattering. Knocking on the doors didn't always go to plan though. Williams was knocked on a door in Ordsall, when a man came to the door naked. Williams said "Hi mate. I am standing for the mayor and was hoping I could count on your vote"

The naked man replied. "Hi I am Tony Keogh. I thought you were the Jehovah's Witnesses I thought if I answered the door like this they wouldn't come again" Williams laughed and said "No, I bet they wouldn't mate. So, now I've seen you naked, can I count on your vote?"

"Yes" said Tony I'll put some clothes on when I go to the polling station though".

There was another door he knocked on was in Weaste, when an old girl had him at it. She said "I would vote for you but I usually go shopping on a Thursday .But if you take me to Tesco on Wednesday I can" . Williams agreed. Why? I don't know as she had him carrying her bags and taking him to her friends. She even had him dropping her off at bingo. When she got out she said to Williams "You are labour aren't you?"

"No" said Williams.

"Oh, you wont be getting my vote then. I always vote labour". Williams was livid and felt like giving her a mouthful but decided against it as it wouldn't look too good. Some days,Williams felt like a double glazing salesman the amount of doors that were slammed in his face.

He was getting very excited as the day was drawing near. In fact he hardly slept a wink the night before the big day , he was so nervous.

The day of the vote arrived. Williams ,had a shower shave and sh. Well, the other thing he did. He was ready for his big day. His campaign manager picked him up at eight thirty. They drove over to his local polling station in Clifton, where he proudly ticked the box next to his name before trying to get as many last minute votes as he could. He was trying right up to the end . He wanted this as much for himself as for the people of Salford. He knew he wouldn't let them down. They went over to the Ordsall polling station, where he spotted Tony Keogh, who fortunately, this time had his clothes on. They shared a joke and shook hands, which strangely they didn't do the last time they met. Williams had been a bit unsure, as to what the Tony Keogh had been up to.

Well, time was getting on and Williams and his party left for the town hall in Swinton to hear the result. They arrived at this fine building at ten to ten. Williams noticed a couple off familiar faces. The first to approach Williams was Tony Flynn from Salford On-line. "Well. How do you think its gone, Simon?".

" Hi Tony " smiled Williams. " I don't think it could of gone much better to tell you the truth. My team deserve the utmost respect for the time and effort they have put in. I couldn't have done it without them. All we can do now is wait. It's down to the public and what they decide"

" Well. good luck my friend" , said Tony.

"Thanks "said Williams.

In the crowd, Williams spotted another friendly face. It was Joe Barnwell from Salford City Radio. He waved Simon over. "Hi Simon. My show was nominated for a Sony award for the interview I did with you and it won"

"Nice one Joe. I bet your buzzing" said Williams with a genuine fondness for this man who had really started this ball rolling.

"Yes I am" said Joe "and by the way, I voted for you".

"Thanks a lot mate" said Williams. It was then that Williams spotted Dianne Dawson. He didn't know what to expect. Their eyes met. She walked over to him and said in that sexy voice " Hi Simon". Williams, for once in his life nearly melted right there on the spot. He looked at her dumbstruck, like the first time he had seen her. "Look Dianne" he said "I am so sorry the way things turned out on that date. I never meant for any of that to happen. It wasn't supposed to turn out like that". Dianne looked at Williams. The spark they had was still there. Dianne purred "I haven't been out with anyone since that date" Williams, for a split second was genuinely moved until she added " I couldn't face another date. I am still in trauma over that weekend"

Williams lowered his head and said "I am really so sorry. I just couldn't help myself when I saw Van Persie. It was brilliant"

"Not for me it wasn't. I even gave your son a detention for it" she replied.

"I know. He told me. So, you're not courting then?"

"No. I just told you. The last date I had was more than enough. I am still having nightmares because of it."

Fortunately for Williams, Dianne was interrupted by the returning officer. "Can all candidates please go to the stage. The results are in"

All the candidates lined up anxiously. Good evening Ladies and Gentlemen. I am Tracey Poyser, returning officer for Salford. Here are the results...

Phil Ratcliffe   LABOUR   19,792
Jimmy Mythen   LIBERAL 7,451
Joanne Riddle   CONSERVATE 11,783
Simon Williams   INDEPENDENT 33, 790
It gives me great pleasure to say the new Mayor for Salford is Simon Williams. The crowd went berserk, whistling and shouting and cheering. Williams stepped up to the microphone to make his first speech as Mayor Of Salford. "I would like to thank all the people of Salford who have taken the time to vote for me. I promise I will do my best for you all .This is the best city in the world and I will do my utmost to prove to people that it is. We are Salford and we can class it up with the best." He left the stage to huge cheers and a lots of hand shakes. He saw Dianne smiling at him and before he could say a word she said " Listen Williams. You know I quite like you. So, if you want we will try again". They kissed tenderly.

Williams had to pinch himself. "I cannot believe it. Today is up there with the top five days in my life Dianne. Oh and by the way , its Mayor Williams now. Come on, let's go home and I'll show you my big shiny chain. Giggling, they walked of hand in hand ………

        THE END ………………
                    OR IS IT ????????